HOCKEY SUPERSTARS

THE LEAFS VS. THE CANADIENS

BY

James Duplacey

Kids Can Press

TORONTO

Kids Can Press Ltd. acknowledges with appreciation the assistance of the Canada Council and the Ontario Arts Council in the production of this book.

Cataloguing in Publication Data

Duplacey, James
          The Leafs vs. the Canadiens: the NHL's top teams

(Hockey superstars)
ISBN 1-55074-358-9

1. Toronto Maple Leafs (Hockey team) — History — Juvenile literature.
2. Montreal Canadiens (Hockey team) — History — Juvenile literature.
3. Hockey — Canada — History — Juvenile literature. I. Title. II. Series.

GV848.T67D8 1996   j796.962'64'0971   C96-931431-0

Kids Can Press Ltd.
29 Birch Avenue
Toronto, Ontario, Canada
M4V 1E2

Edited by Elizabeth MacLeod
Book design and electronic page layout by First Image
Printed and bound in Canada

96 0 9 8 7 6 5 4 3 2 1

Photo credits
Harold Barkley Archives: 13 (centre middle). **Bruce Bennett Studios:** front cover (foreground left and right), 3 (second from right), 5 (top right), 8 (all), 9 (all), 10 (left), 11 (top right), 12 (bottom right), 13 (top left and middle, bottom right), 16 (top right, bottom right), 17 (top left, middle right), 19 (top left), 21 (bottom right), 23 (top right, bottom left), 24 (all), 25 (all), 26 (top left and right, bottom right), 28 (bottom right), 29 (top left and middle, bottom middle and right), 30 (all), 31 (all), back cover (middle). **Denis Brodeur:** 3 (left), 11 (top left), 13 (bottom left and middle), 23 (bottom right), 27 (top right). **Michael Burns:** 29 (centre right). **Canada Wide Feature Service:** front cover (background top middle), 7 (bottom right). **Graphic Artists / Hockey Hall of Fame:** front cover (background bottom left), 5 (bottom right), 12 (bottom middle), 13 (centre right), 14 (right), 15 (top left), 19 (bottom left), 27 (bottom right), 28 (bottom middle). **Hockey Hall of Fame:** 6 (left), 7 (middle, bottom left), 12 (top middle, bottom left), 13 (top right), 15 (bottom middle), 27 (bottom left), 28 (top middle), 29 (top right). **Imperial Oil Turofsky Collection / Hockey Hall of Fame:** front cover (background top left), 3 (second from left), 4 (top), 6 (right), 10 (bottom left), 11 (top right),13 (centre left), 14 (left), 15 (top middle), 16 (left), 18 (left, right), 20 (all), 21 (top right), 22 (both), 27 (top left), 28 (bottom left), 29 (centre left and middle). **Doug MacLellan / Hockey Hall of Fame:** front cover (background top right), 5 (top left, bottom left), 21 (middle right), back cover (left). **Frank Prazak / Hockey Hall of Fame:** front cover (background bottom middle and right), 3 (right), 4 (middle), 7 (top right), 15 (right), 17 (bottom left), 18 (bottom, middle), 19 (right, middle), 21 (left), 23 (top left), 26 (bottom left), 28 (top right), 29 (bottom left), back cover (right).

CONTENTS

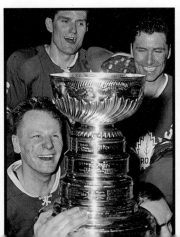
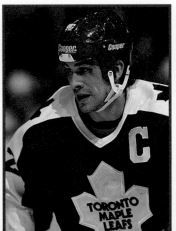

Go Team Go!

As the arena lights dim, the Montreal Canadiens and Toronto Maple Leafs skate onto the ice. The fans rise to greet their heroes, and there are as many Leafs sweaters as Canadiens jerseys in the crowd. It's almost impossible to tell where the game is being played. And that's what makes any game between these teams so special. When the Leafs and Habs meet, time and place are unimportant. This is hockey at its best. This is the greatest rivalry in the history of the NHL.

The rivalry is province against province, blue against red, and neighbour against neighbour. It's today's heroes, such as Wendel Clark and Doug Gilmour, Jocelyn Thibault and Vincent Damphousse. And it's the spirit of yesterday's stars, including Guy Lafleur and Darryl Sittler, "Rocket" Richard and Ted "Teeder" Kennedy. The names may change, but the heart of the game stays the same.

The great moments in Habs and Leafs games, the all-star performances and the on-ice heroes of hockey's greatest rivalry — you'll find them all right here on these pages.

Rocket Richard holds the Habs record for most goals, and Turk Broda owns the Maple Leafs record for most shutouts. This is how they looked in 1947 when they did battle.

Habs captain Jean Béliveau and Leafs Bob Pulford always made sparks fly when the two teams met.

When the Habs won the Stanley Cup four times in a row between 1976 and 1979, Bob Gainey was an important member of the club.

The NHL's greatest rivalry continues today with top players such as Leafs Mats Sundin and Canadiens Pierre Turgeon.

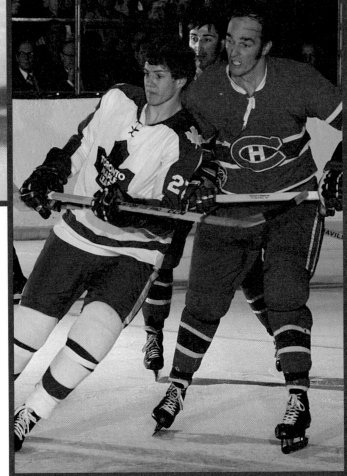

Martin Rucinsky of the Habs screens Leafs netminder Felix Potvin as he tries for a tip-in goal.

Darryl Sittler holds the records for most goals (389) and most points (916) scored by a Maple Leaf.

HISTORY OF THE RIVALRY

The Montreal Canadiens franchise began in 1910, even before there was a National Hockey League. When the NHL was formed in 1917–18, the Canadiens became one of the first teams to join, along with a team from Toronto called the Arenas. The Arenas changed their name to the St. Patricks in 1919, then became the Maple Leafs in 1927.

In their first 20 seasons in the NHL, the Canadiens' main rival was the Montreal Maroons. The teams played in the same rink, the Forum, and when they met each other there, it was a high-tension clash. But the Maroons folded in 1938, leaving just two Canadian teams, Montreal and Toronto. It was only natural that they should become fierce enemies. When Dick Irvin quit as coach of the Leafs to join the Canadiens in 1940, it only added to that rivalry.

The Leafs-Habs rivalry was at its hottest between 1942 and 1967. There were only six teams in the NHL back then, so the two teams played each other 14 times each season. When they met, the hockey was fast and exciting because Montreal and Toronto were known as the best teams with the top players.

As well, fans could almost always tune into a Leafs or Habs game since the teams dominated radio and television. Add to this the fact that the cities of Montreal and Toronto were always competing to be the biggest and best in Canada, and it's no wonder that their hockey teams were arch-rivals.

Playoff meetings between the Habs and Leafs have made the rivalry even hotter, and the two teams have played each other often enough to make the sparks really fly. From 1944 to 1967 Toronto and Montreal met 11 times in the playoffs. Five times, the Stanley Cup was on the line. Many of the games were on-ice wars, famous for some of the greatest moments in hockey history.

Before the Toronto Maple Leafs, there were the Toronto Arenas and the Toronto St. Pats. The Arenas won the Stanley Cup in 1918.

Maple Leaf Gardens, home of the Toronto Maple Leafs, in the 1940s.

Since 1967, the teams have met in the playoffs twice, with Montreal winning both battles. Those wins gave the Habs fans an edge on the suffering Leafs supporters. But when Pat Burns left the Canadiens to coach the Leafs, it really steamed the Habs fans. The first meeting of the two teams with Burns behind the Leafs bench was the highlight of the 1992–93 season. And Leafs-Habs games continue to be the high points of every hockey fan's season.

The Canadiens won the Stanley Cup finals in four straight games in 1968.

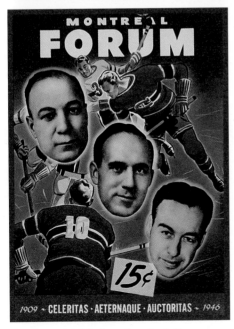

The Habs hoisted coach Dick Irvin onto their shoulders after they won the Stanley Cup in 1953.

Three in a row! The Leafs were one happy team in 1964, when they won the Stanley Cup for the third straight season.

Back in 1946, here's what the programs looked like at the Habs' old arena, the Forum. Now they play at the Molson Centre.

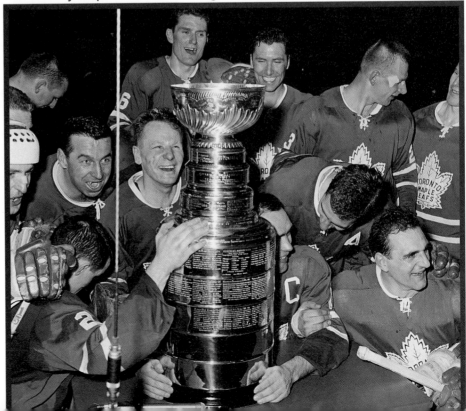

TODAY'S TOP FORWARDS

Wendel Clark

Left Wing — Toronto, Quebec, NY Islanders

No one has worn the Maple Leaf with more pride than Wendel Clark. Clark became one of the most popular Leaf players of all time with his energetic style and thundering bodychecks. He still shares the Leaf record for goals by a rookie.

Martin Rucinsky

Left Wing — Edmonton, Quebec, Colorado, Montreal

Martin Rucinsky quickly won the hearts of Habs fans with his hard-working style. He has quick hands, a bullet wrist shot and lots of heart. And Rucinsky is not afraid to drive to the net for rebounds or tip-ins.

Doug Gilmour

Centre — St. Louis, Calgary, Toronto

Since arriving in Toronto in 1992, Doug Gilmour has become the heart of the Leafs. He knows only one way to play the game: all out, all the time. Whether he's killing penalties, directing power plays or taking key face-offs, Gilmour always gives his full effort.

Vincent Damphousse

Left Wing — Toronto, Edmonton, Montreal

Vincent Damphousse was the only member of the 1995–96 Montreal Canadiens to have also played for Toronto. His smooth skating and slick passing helped him become the first player to lead three different teams in scoring in three consecutive seasons.

Mats Sundin

Centre — Quebec, Toronto

An agile skater with a wicked wrist shot, Mats Sundin has led the Leafs in scoring in each of his first two seasons. Skilled at playing both centre and wing, Sundin can deke a defender with a quick head fake or elude him with a sudden burst of speed.

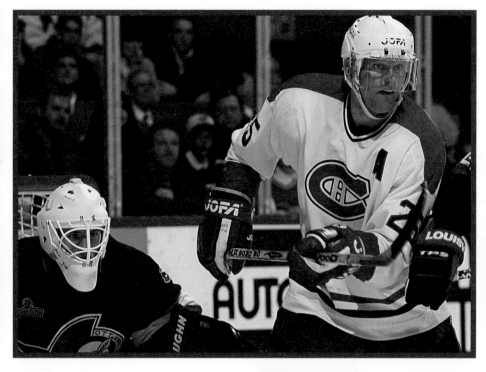

Pierre Turgeon

Centre — Buffalo, NY Islanders, Montreal

A fan favourite and a two-time 100-point scorer, Pierre Turgeon became the 24th captain of the Canadiens in October 1995. Turgeon is a top scorer thanks to his remarkable playmaking skill and the fact that he actually moves much faster than he seems to be moving.

Famous Moments in Leafs History

Sittler's Perfect Ten: 1976

On February 7, 1976, Darryl Sittler set a record that may never be broken. The Leaf captain scored six goals and added four assists for an NHL-record ten points in a single game. He also became the seventh player ever in NHL history to score six goals in a game.

Bobby Baun's Broken Bones: 1964

Late in game six of the Leafs–Red Wings Stanley Cup final, Bobby Baun took a shot on the ankle and was carried off the ice. But he came back and scored the winning goal in overtime. He helped the Leafs win their third Cup in a row — later it was found that Baun had broken his ankle!

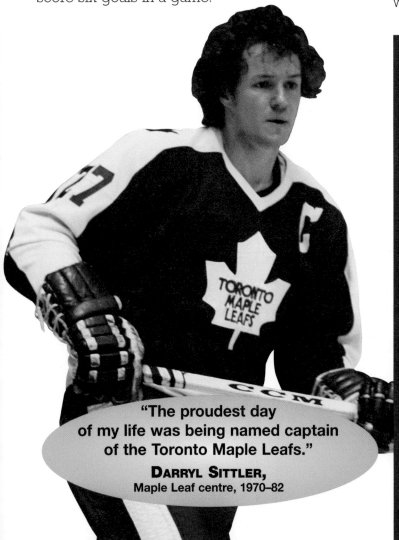

"The proudest day of my life was being named captain of the Toronto Maple Leafs."

DARRYL SITTLER,
Maple Leaf centre, 1970–82

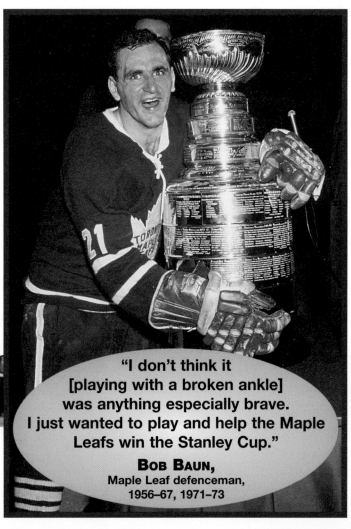

"I don't think it [playing with a broken ankle] was anything especially brave. I just wanted to play and help the Maple Leafs win the Stanley Cup."

BOB BAUN,
Maple Leaf defenceman, 1956–67, 1971–73

Ya Gotta Love Lanny: 1978

In game seven of the 1978 Islanders-Leafs quarter-final series, Lanny McDonald showed why he was one of the most popular Leafs ever. Despite a broken jaw, Lanny scored the series-winning goal in overtime. That goal put the Leafs into the semi-finals for the first time since 1967.

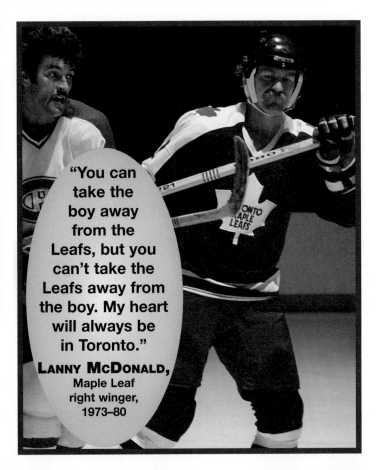

"You can take the boy away from the Leafs, but you can't take the Leafs away from the boy. My heart will always be in Toronto."

LANNY McDONALD,
Maple Leaf
right winger,
1973–80

Gilmour's Glitter: 1993

Doug Gilmour did it all for the Leafs in 1992–93. He set team records for assists (95) and points (127) in a season. Gilmour played with intensity and courage, igniting the offence and helping direct the defence. That leadership won him the Selke Trophy as top defensive forward in 1993.

The Comeback Kids: 1942

In the 1942 Stanley Cup finals, the Maple Leafs performed a miracle. After losing the first three games of the series to Detroit, the Leafs stormed back to win the final four games. No team in any sport has ever rebounded from being behind three games to none to win a championship final.

ALL-TIME BEST DEFENCEMEN

Every hockey expert knows that a team needs great defence to win the Stanley Cup. Toronto and Montreal have won 37 Cup championships between them, so it's obvious that some of the game's finest defencemen have played for these clubs. Here they are, arranged according to the decades in which they played.

★ 1930s ★
Sylvio Mantha

★ Played on three Stanley Cup–winning teams
★ Scored 135 points in 538 career games with Montreal
★ Twice NHL Second All-Star Team

★ 1940s ★
Emile "Butch" Bouchard

★ Four-time NHL All-Star defenceman
★ Captain of Canadiens from 1948 to 1956
★ Played entire 15-year career with Montreal

★ 1950s ★
Doug Harvey

★ Won Norris Trophy seven times
★ Led all NHL defencemen in assists three times
★ Played on six Stanley Cup–winning teams

★ 1960s ★
Jacques Laperriere

★ Won Calder Trophy in 1963–64
★ Won Norris Trophy in 1965–66
★ Played on six Stanley Cup–winning teams

★ 1970s ★
Larry Robinson

★ Won Norris Trophy in 1976–77 and 1979–80
★ Second-highest season plus/minus in history (plus 120)
★ Three-time NHL First Team All-Star

★ 1980s ★
Chris Chelios

★ Won Norris Trophy in 1988–89
★ Played on 1986 Stanley Cup–winning team
★ Member of NHL All-Rookie Team in 1984–85

★ 1990s ★
Eric Desjardins

★ First defenceman to score a hat trick in Cup finals
★ Led all Habs defencemen in scoring in 1992–93
★ Scored career-high 13 goals in 1992–93

★ 1930s ★
Frank "King" Clancy

★ Led all Leaf defencemen in scoring six times
★ Twice NHL First Team All-Star
★ Twice NHL Second Team All-Star

★ 1940s ★
Walter "Babe" Pratt

★ Won Hart Trophy in 1943–44
★ Shares team record for assists in one game (6)
★ Recorded career-high 57 points in 1943–44

★ 1950s ★
Jimmy Thomson

★ Played on four Stanley Cup–winning teams
★ Led all Leaf defencemen in scoring five times
★ Captain of Maple Leafs in 1956–57

★ 1960s ★
Tim Horton

★ Known as "the strongest man in hockey"
★ Holds Leaf record for consecutive games played (486)
★ Three-time NHL First Team All-Star

★ 1970s ★
Ian Turnbull

★ Holds NHL record for goals in game by defenceman (5)
★ Set team record for points in one season by defenceman (79)
★ Only Leaf defenceman with back-to-back 20-goal seasons

★ 1980s ★
Borje Salming

★ Leafs' all-time leader in assists (620)
★ Six straight NHL All-Star Team selections
★ Holds team records for goals, assists and points by defenceman

★ 1990s ★
Dave Ellett

★ Set Leaf record for playoff points by defenceman (18)
★ Set Leaf record for playoff assists by defenceman (14)
★ Led all Leaf defencemen in goals and points in 1991–92

THE HALL OF FAME

More players from the Montreal Canadiens and Toronto Maple Leafs have been elected to the Hockey Hall of Fame than from any other teams. A total of 75 Montreal and Toronto players have received this honour. You can see all their names on the inside covers of this book as well as the year each joined the Hall of Fame. Here are six of those superstars who played for both teams.

Bert Olmstead

Elected to the Hall of Fame 1985

One of the NHL's all-time great playmakers, Bert Olmstead won four Stanley Cup titles with Montreal and one with Toronto. He was an extremely accurate passer and he led the NHL in assists twice. When he joined the Leafs in 1958, he was also made an assistant coach.

Frank Mahovlich

Elected to the Hall of Fame 1981

Frank Mahovlich had two very distinct careers. In Toronto, he was the team's top gun and led the Leafs in goals for six straight seasons. In Montreal "the Big M" was the club's best playmaker, leading the Habs in assists in each of his three full seasons with the team. Mahovlich won the Stanley Cup with both teams, four times as a Leaf and twice more as a Canadien.

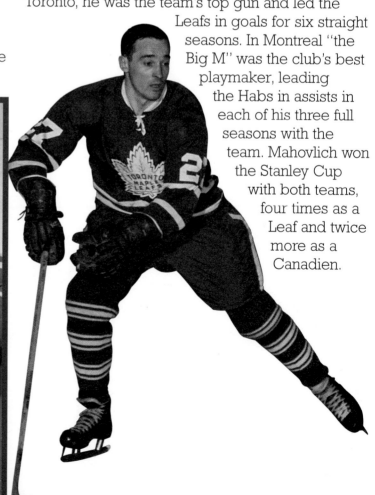

Dickie Moore

Elected to the Hall of Fame 1974

For two seasons in the 1950s, Dickie Moore was the NHL's top scorer. This Montreal star was a super passer and shooter. In 1957–58 he led the NHL in goals and points. The next season, he led in assists and points. Moore retired in 1963, but returned to the NHL with the Leafs in 1964.

Gordie Drillon

Elected to the Hall of Fame 1975

Gordie Drillon was the NHL's top tip-in artist. From the edge of the crease, he would deflect pucks past the goalie. How good was Drillon? He led the Leafs in goals in four of his six years with the team. When he joined Montreal in 1942–43 he had his best goals total ever.

Jacques Plante

Elected to the Hall of Fame 1978

Between 1955 and 1960, Jacques Plante led the Canadiens to five straight Stanley Cup wins. When he joined Toronto in 1970 at the age of 41 he was the oldest goalie still playing in the NHL. But Plante led the league with a goals-against average of 1.88 — the second-lowest GAA of his career!

George Hainsworth

Elected to the Hall of Fame 1961

In 1928–29 George Hainsworth recorded 22 shutouts for Montreal. Now, that's a record that will never be broken! No goalie could move across the net as fast as he could. He was also one of the first goalies to "stack the pads" to stop shots. He joined the Leafs in 1933.

FAMOUS MOMENTS IN CANADIENS HISTORY

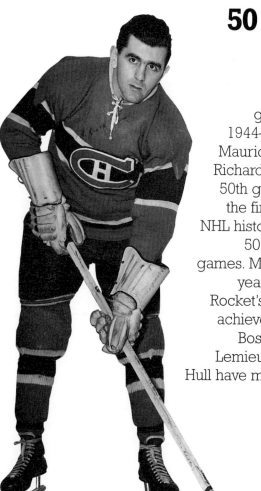

50 in 50: 1945

In the last game of the 1944–45 season, Maurice "Rocket" Richard scored his 50th goal. He was the first player in NHL history to score 50 goals in 50 games. More than 50 years since the Rocket's incredible achievement, only Bossy, Gretzky, Lemieux and Brett Hull have matched this record.

Lemieux for Two: 1986

The 1986 Montreal Canadiens were not supposed to win the Stanley Cup. After all, they had nine rookies on the team. But in the opening series against Hartford, rookie Claude Lemieux scored two overtime goals, including the series winner, to down the Whalers. Montreal ended up winning the Cup.

"The goal against Hartford was one I worked so hard for. It is the kind of goal I wish someone would make a tape of to show my kids."

CLAUDE LEMIEUX,
Canadiens right winger, 1983–90

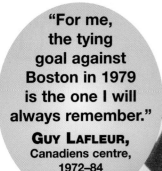

"For me, the tying goal against Boston in 1979 is the one I will always remember."

GUY LAFLEUR,
Canadiens centre,
1972–84

Lafleur's Legacy: 1979

The biggest goal of Guy Lafleur's career came against Boston in game seven of the 1979 semi-finals. The Bruins were leading 4–3 with less than two minutes left. Then they received a penalty for having too many men on the ice. Lafleur tied the game, Montreal won in overtime and went on to win their fourth straight Stanley Cup.

"Playing on the Montreal Canadiens in the 1970s, we knew we had to win the Stanley Cup. If we lost out in the finals, that wasn't good enough. We had to win."

KEN DRYDEN,
Canadiens goaltender,
1971–73, 1974–79

Stick It to 'Em: 1993

In the 1993 finals, the Habs lost game one to Los Angeles and were down a goal late in game two. But then Kings defenceman Marty McSorley was caught with an illegal stick and Montreal was awarded a power play. The Habs tied the game, then won it in overtime and went on to win their 24th Stanley Cup.

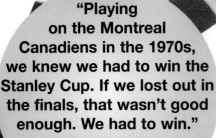

Dryden's Debut: 1971

Late in the 1970–71 season, Ken Dryden made his NHL debut. The rookie won all six starts he made for the Habs. Then he went on to lead the Canadiens to the Stanley Cup championship. Dryden's heroics made him the first rookie to win the playoff MVP award.

DID YOU KNOW ...

★ ... Red Kelly (above) was a Member of Parliament while he was playing for the Maple Leafs? He won in the suburban Toronto riding of York West in 1962.

★ ... Hector "Toe" Blake of the Habs is the only player ever to score a Stanley Cup–winning goal, serve as a Stanley Cup–winning captain and coach a Stanley Cup–winning team?

★ ... Canadiens hotshot Bernie "Boom Boom" Geoffrion (right) perfected the slapshot and used it to score 50 goals in a single season?

★ ... until Todd Gill was traded to San Jose, he was the longest-serving Leaf defenceman since Borje Salming? Gill played in 639 games, which ranks him fifth among all Leaf rearguards.

★ ... Henri Richard played on an NHL-record 11 Stanley Cup–winning teams? "The Pocket Rocket" played on his first winning team in 1956 and his last in 1973 — all with the Canadiens.

★ ... Leafs coach George "Punch" Imlach (below) was the first NHL coach to win the Stanley Cup four times without ever playing in the league?

⭐ ... George Armstrong (below, right) served longer as captain of the Maple Leafs than any other player? "The Chief" was captain of the Leafs from 1957 to 1969.

⭐ ... on November 5, 1955, Jean Béliveau scored three goals in 44 seconds, all on the same power play? Until the start of the 1956–57 season, a penalized player had to serve his entire penalty even if the other team scored.

⭐ ... Rick Vaive (below) was the first Leaf to score 50 goals in a season? "Squid" reached the 50-goal plateau in three straight seasons.

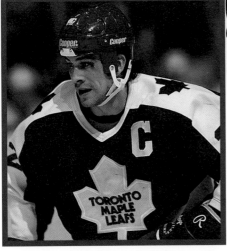

⭐ ... Yvan Cournoyer (below) was the last Montreal Canaldiens player to score five goals in a game? He notched five markers against the Chicago Black Hawks on February 15, 1975.

⭐ ... Jacques Lemaire (above), Toe Blake, Jean Béliveau, Henri Richard and Howie Morenz each scored two Stanley Cup–winning goals?

⭐ ... the CH on the Canadiens jersey stands for Club de Hockey Canadien? The nickname "Habs" is short for *habitants*, which refers to the first settlers in Quebec.

⭐ ... Darryl Sittler is the only Leaf to score a goal with the team two men short? Sittler scored against Winnipeg on March 19, 1980, while both Ian Turnbull and Pat Hickey were in the penalty box.

⭐ ... six former Leafs went on to become NHL referees after they retired? Francis "King" Clancy, Art Duncan, Clarence "Hap" Day, Cecil "Babe" Dye, Melville "Butch" Keeling and Gaye Stewart were all referees in the NHL.

⭐ ... when Conn Smythe took over the Toronto St. Pats he changed the name to the Maple Leafs to honour the Maple Leaf Regiment, an army unit that fought for Canada in World War I?

GREAT GOALIES, PAST AND PRESENT

Bill Durnan

Montreal

Bill Durnan's love of baseball improved his reflexes and balance, and helped keep him square to the shooter. Durnan could also shoot and catch left- and right-handed. He would switch his stick from hand to hand so that he always had his catching hand protecting the wide side of the net.

Walter "Turk" Broda

Toronto

Turk Broda was at his best when the pressure was on. Other goalies may have had better statistics during the regular season, but no one outplayed Broda in the playoffs. He guided the Leafs to five Stanley Cup wins and led all playoff goalies in shutouts in each of those championship seasons.

Jacques Plante

Montreal, NY Rangers, St. Louis, Toronto, Boston

Jacques Plante introduced the mask to hockey and was the first goalie to stop the puck behind the net and dive out of the net to smother rebounds. He led the league in goals-against average eight times, won the Vezina Trophy seven times and played on six Cup-winning teams in Montreal.

Johnny Bower

NY Rangers, Toronto

Johnny Bower played in the NHL until he was 45 years old — and he rarely wore a mask. This goalie perfected the poke-check: he would dive out of the net and knock the puck off the opponent's stick. That style helped Bower lead the Leafs to four Stanley Cup titles.

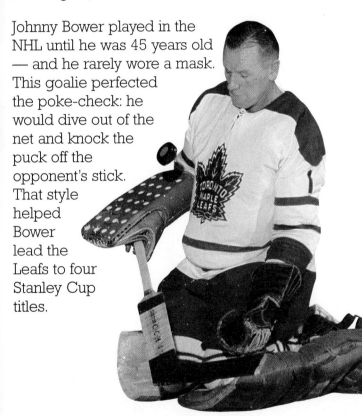

Felix Potvin

Toronto

He's nicknamed "the Cat" because of his fast reflexes. Felix Potvin is so good because he can block the bottom of the net with his pads and body, and use his quick glove hand to protect the top. As a rookie, Potvin led the NHL in goals-against average and he has already played in two All-Star games.

Patrick Roy

Montreal, Colorado

Many goalies have copied Patrick Roy's style, but Roy perfected the butterfly style of dropping to his knees with his pads in a V. His leg strength, balance and positioning made him the best goalie of the 1980s. Roy won 11 awards and two Stanley Cup titles while with the Habs.

FAMOUS LEAFS - HABS GAMES

The first game between the Montreal Canadiens and the Toronto Maple Leafs was played at the Mutual Street Arena in Toronto on February 24, 1927. The Habs downed the Leafs 3–2. Since that time, these two teams have played some of the all-time great games in NHL history.

March 23, 1944:
Montreal 5, Toronto 1

In 1944 the Leafs and Canadiens met for the first time in the playoffs. During game two of the semi-finals, Rocket Richard scored all five goals as the Canadiens raked the Leafs 5–1. He was just the second NHL player to score five times in a playoff game. Broadcaster Foster Hewitt named Richard the game's first, second and third stars, the only time in NHL history that has happened. Richard was still scoring on the Leafs in 1960 (below).

April 21, 1951:
Toronto 3, Montreal 2 (OT)

Every game of the 1951 Stanley Cup finals between Montreal and Toronto went into overtime. Early in the first overtime period of the fifth and final game, Leaf rearguard Bill Barilko backhanded the puck past Gerry McNeil to give the Leafs their fourth Cup title in five years. That made Barilko the first NHL defenceman to score a Stanley Cup–winning goal. Sadly, Barilko was killed in a plane crash later that summer.

April 25, 1967:
Toronto 3, Montreal 2

Canada's 100th birthday was in 1967, so it seemed fitting that the Leafs and Canadiens should meet in the Stanley Cup finals. Game three featured the longest overtime game ever between the two teams. In the second overtime period, Bob Pulford scored to win the game for the Leafs. Toronto was called "the Old Pappies" because the team had 15 players over the age of 30, but they still went on to win the Stanley Cup.

January 9, 1993:
Toronto 5, Montreal 4

There was something very special about the Leafs-Habs match-up of January 9, 1993. That was the night former Montreal coach Pat Burns returned to the Forum — behind the bench of the Maple Leafs! All in the crowd were on the edge of their seats. Even though they were playing their fourth game in six nights, the Leafs had

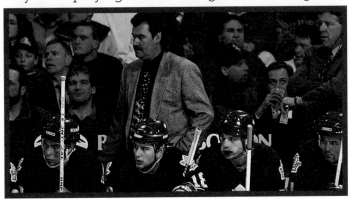

plenty of energy left for the Habs. They downed Montreal for their first win at the Forum since October 17, 1988.

April 22, 1979:
Montreal 4,
Toronto 3 (OT)

The rivalry between the Leafs and Habs was renewed in 1979 in game three of the quarter-finals. The Habs held a 2–1 lead until late in the game, when Darryl

Sittler tied it up. The teams battled through 25 minutes of overtime before Cam Connor (below) won it for the Canadiens. Mike Palmateer (above) was the hero for Toronto, making 45 saves in a losing cause. Montreal swept the series and went on to win their fourth straight Stanley Cup.

TODAY'S TOP DEFENCEMEN

Larry Murphy

Los Angeles, Washington, Minnesota, Pittsburgh, Toronto

Even though he's played 16 seasons and won two Stanley Cup titles, Larry Murphy is not well known. That's because this quiet superstar leads by example, not by words. Murphy has the knowledge and skills to mount a rush, clear the crease and dig the puck from the corners.

Lyle Odelein

Montreal

Lyle Odelein plays defence the old-fashioned way — with his body. Odelein is solid on his skates, so it's hard to knock him off the puck. He's also versatile: when he was asked to play forward in 1993–94, he responded by scoring six power-play goals!

Mathieu Schneider

Montreal, NY Islanders, Toronto

What sets Mathieu Schneider apart from other players is his focus. He can visualize where the open passing lanes are and where the opposing forwards might attack. That allows him to be in position to set up a teammate or break up an opponent's scoring chance.

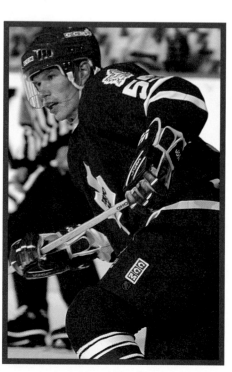

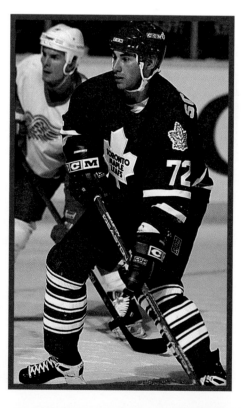

Vladimir Malakhov

NY Islanders, Montreal

Vladimir Malakhov has always had offensive ability, but he's improved his defensive skills while playing in Montreal. He's learned to use his size to play strong positional defence and his strength to dish out bone-rattling bodychecks. Malakhov has become one of the top Canadiens rearguards.

Dave Ellett

Winnipeg, Toronto

Dave Ellett has been a creative leader and solid defender for the Leafs ever since he was acquired from Winnipeg in 1990. Known for his fluid skating and artistic playmaking, Ellett has led all Leaf defencemen in assists in four of his six seasons with the team.

Patrice Brisebois

Montreal

The Canadiens "take-charge" leader on the blue line, Patrice Brisebois keys the offence with his creative playmaking and anchors the defence with his solid positional play. This six-year NHL veteran has improved every year and he had his finest season in 1995–96.

AWARD WINNERS

Four of the NHL's top trophies have connections to the Montreal Canadiens and Toronto Maple Leafs. The Hart, Selke, Conn Smythe and Vezina awards are presented in memory of individuals who played central roles in the success of Canada's greatest teams. You'll find the names of all the Habs and Leafs who have won NHL awards on page 32.

Conn Smythe Trophy

This trophy was donated to the NHL by former Leaf owner Conn Smythe to salute the most valuable player in the playoffs. Jean Béliveau scored eight goals in the 1965 playoffs to earn the first-ever Conn Smythe Trophy award. Since then, seven other Habs have been honoured, including Serge Savard (left). Patrick Roy is the only Canadiens player to win the award twice. The only Maple Leaf to win the Conn Smythe is Dave Keon (below). His grit and desire earned him the award in 1967.

Frank J. Selke Trophy

Frank Selke was the first assistant general manager of the Maple Leafs. Then in 1946 he became the general manager of the Canadiens and guided them to six Stanley Cup titles. Selke's teams always featured forwards who played tough defence. So this trophy honours each season's best defensive forward.

It's only fitting that the Habs have dominated this trophy. Bob Gainey won it in four straight seasons. Guy Carbonneau (above), another Canadiens captain, has earned it three times. Maple Leaf Doug Gilmour (right) was the first player to record 100 points in the same season he won the award.

Hart Memorial Trophy

This trophy was donated in 1923 by Dr. David Hart. He was the father of Cecil Hart, who was a manager-coach of the Canadiens. The trophy rewards the NHL's most valuable player. Eleven Montreal Canadiens, including Jean Beliveau (right), have won the Hart Trophy and every one has been inducted into the Hockey Hall of Fame. Jacques Plante won the award in 1961–62 and no goalie has won it since. The Leafs who have won this trophy are Ted Kennedy (below) and Walter "Babe" Pratt.

Vezina Trophy

Georges Vezina (left) never missed a game in his 15 years with the Canadiens. But in the first game of the 1925–26 season, he became ill and never played again. When Vezina died later that season, the Canadiens owners dedicated a trophy to the best goaltender in his honour.

George Hainsworth replaced Vezina in 1926–27 and won the Vezina Trophy in his first three years in the league. Habs goalies Bill Durnan, Jacques Plante, Ken Dryden, Michel "Bunny" Larocque and Patrick Roy also won the Vezina at least three times. Maple Leaf netminders Walter "Turk" Broda and Johnny Bower (right) each took home the trophy twice.

ALL-TIME BEST FORWARDS

Flashy scorers and rugged checkers have played centre or winger for the Canadiens and the Leafs. Forwards from both teams have been named most valuable player, best defensive forward and top playoff performer in the NHL. You can meet some of the top ones here — they're arranged according to the decades in which they played.

★ 1930s ★
Howie Morenz

★ Led NHL in goals, assists and points in 1927–28

★ Scored two Stanley Cup–winning goals

★ Notched 256 goals and 412 points for Montreal

★ 1940s ★
Elmer Lach

★ Led NHL in assists three times

★ Won Art Ross Trophy in 1944–45 and 1947–1948

★ First Canadien to record 600 points

★ 1950s ★
Maurice "Rocket" Richard

★ First player to score 50 goals in 50 games

★ Led NHL in goals scored five times

★ Holds NHL record for playoff over-time goals (6)

★ 1960s ★
Jean Béliveau

★ First winner of Conn Smythe Trophy

★ Played on ten Stanley Cup–winning teams

★ Led NHL in goals twice

★ 1970s ★
Guy Lafleur

★ Scored at least 50 goals in six straight seasons

★ Recorded at least 100 points in six straight seasons

★ Won Hart Trophy in 1976–77 and 1977–78

★ 1980s ★
Bob Gainey

★ Won Selke Trophy four years in a row (1978–81)

★ Won Conn Smythe Trophy in 1978–79

★ Captain of Canadiens from 1981 to 1989

★ 1990s ★
Vincent Damphousse

★ Led Montreal in scoring in 1992–93 and 1993–94

★ Scored at least 30 goals in five seasons

★ Recorded career-high 97 points in 1992–93

★ 1930s ★
Charlie Conacher

★ Held or shared NHL title for top goal-scorer five times

★ Won Art Ross Trophy in 1933–34 and 1934–35

★ Five-time NHL All-Star

★ 1940s ★
Syl Apps

★ Led NHL in assists in 1936–37 and 1937–38

★ Won Calder Trophy in 1936–37

★ Won Lady Byng Trophy in 1941–42

★ 1950s ★
Ted "Teeder" Kennedy

★ Tied for NHL lead in assists in 1950–51

★ Led all playoff scorers in goals (8) and points (14) in 1948

★ Five Stanley Cup wins, three-time All-Star

★ 1960s ★
Frank Mahovlich

★ Won Calder Trophy in 1957–58

★ Set Leaf record for goals (48) in 1960–61

★ Won Cup four times with Leafs and twice with Canadiens

★ 1970s ★
Darryl Sittler

★ Set NHL record with ten points in one game

★ Tied NHL record with five goals in one playoff game

★ All-time Leaf leader in goals (389) and points (916)

★ 1980s ★
Wendel Clark

★ Only Leaf to be chosen first overall in NHL Entry Draft

★ Set Leaf record for goals by a rookie (34)

★ Named to NHL All-Rookie Team in 1985–86

★ 1990s ★
Doug Gilmour

★ Won Selke Trophy in 1992–93

★ Holds Leaf record for points in a season (127)

★ Set Leaf record for points in playoffs (35)

UP-AND-COMERS

Saku Koivu

Centre — Montreal

This swift-skating centre has already made an impression on Montreal fans. Saku Koivu skates with grace and ease and his passes are sharp and accurate. He led all Montreal Canadiens rookies in scoring in 1995–96.

Valeri Bure

Right Wing — Montreal

Valeri Bure has the speed and talent to become an NHL star. Like his famous brother Pavel, this skilled puckhandler and passer is also very efficient in the defensive zone.

David Wilkie

Defence — Montreal

The Habs have high hopes for rookie rearguard David Wilkie. He has size and strength and he's not afraid of the rough going. He also knows when to jump into the play and when to stay back and protect his own zone.

Todd Warriner

Left Wing — Toronto

The play of Todd Warriner was a pleasant surprise for the Maple Leafs in 1995–96. Warriner is best known as a playmaker, but he has also shown the ability to score key goals. In junior he was named an OHL All-Star in 1992 and was a member of the Canadian Olympic Team that played in the 1994 games in Lillehammer, Norway.

Brandon Convery

Centre — Toronto

Scouts for the Maple Leafs liked Brandon Convery's size and strength when they made this centre the eighth junior player chosen in the 1992 Entry Draft. On the ice, Convery is at his best in the slot. He can control the puck well and is an expert at tipping shots past the goalie. With his mobility and his hard, accurate shot, Convery should be in the big time for a long time.

Mark Kolesar

Left Wing — Toronto

Mark Kolesar was never drafted despite three seasons of junior hockey with the Brandon Wheat Kings. Instead, the Leafs signed him as a free agent in 1994 and sent him to their farm team to work on his game. The hard work paid off for Kolesar. This defensive forward has seen only limited ice time, but he has been used in key penalty-killing situations. If Kolesar continues to improve, he'll earn a regular role.

STATISTICS AND RECORDS

TORONTO MAPLE LEAFS

Stanley Cup Championships
1918*, 1922**, 1932, 1942, 1945, 1947, 1948, 1949, 1951, 1962, 1963, 1964, 1967
* as the Toronto Arenas
** as the Toronto St. Pats

AWARD WINNERS

Hart Memorial Trophy
(for most valuable player)
Walter "Babe" Pratt — 1944
Ted Kennedy — 1955

Art Ross Trophy
(for top-scoring player)
Cecil "Babe" Dye — 1923, 1925
Irvine "Ace" Bailey — 1929
Harvey "Busher" Jackson — 1932
Charlie Conacher — 1934, 1935
Gordie Drillon — 1938

Vezina Trophy (for top goalie)
Turk Broda — 1941, 1948
Al Rollins — 1951
Harry Lumley — 1954
Johnny Bower — 1961, 1965
Terry Sawchuk — 1965

Calder Memorial Trophy
(for top rookie)
Syl Apps — 1937
Gaye Stewart — 1943
Gus Bodnar — 1944
Frank McCool — 1945
Howie Meeker — 1947
Frank Mahovlich — 1958
Dave Keon — 1962
Kent Douglas — 1963
Brit Selby — 1966

Conn Smythe Trophy
(for most valuable player in the playoffs)
Dave Keon — 1967

Lady Byng Memorial Trophy (for most gentlemanly player)
Joe Primeau — 1932
Gordie Drillon — 1938
Syl Apps — 1942
Sid Smith — 1952, 1955
Red Kelly — 1961
Dave Keon — 1962, 1963

Frank J. Selke Trophy
(for top defensive forward)
Doug Gilmour — 1993

Jack Adams Award (for top coach)
Pat Burns — 1993

SELECTED RECORD HOLDERS
Team Career Records
Most games: George Armstrong (1187)
Most goals: Darryl Sittler (389)
Most assists: Borje Salming (620)
Most points: Darryl Sittler (916)
Most shutouts: Turk Broda (62)

Team Season Records
Most goals: Rick Vaive (54)
Most assists: Doug Gilmour (95)
Most points: Doug Gilmour (127)
Most shutouts: Harry Lumley (13)

NHL Records
Most points, one game: Darryl Sittler (10)
Most goals, one game, defenceman: Ian Turnbull (5)
Most goals, one game, rookie: Howie Meeker (5)
Most assists, one game, defenceman: Babe Pratt (6)
Most goals, one period: Busher Jackson (4)
Most goals, one playoff game: Darryl Sittler (5)
Most goals, final series: Babe Dye (9)

MONTREAL CANADIENS

Stanley Cup Championships
1916*, 1924, 1930, 1931, 1944, 1946, 1953, 1956, 1957, 1958, 1959, 1960, 1965, 1966, 1968, 1969, 1971, 1973, 1976, 1977, 1978, 1979, 1986, 1993
* won before the creation of the NHL

AWARD WINNERS

Hart Memorial Trophy
(for most valuable player)
Herb Gardiner — 1927
Howie Morenz — 1928, 1931, 1932
Aurel Joliat — 1934
Albert "Babe" Siebert — 1937
Hector "Toe" Blake — 1939
Elmer Lach — 1945
Maurice Richard — 1947
Jean Béliveau — 1956, 1964
Bernie "Boom Boom" Geoffrion — 1961
Jacques Plante — 1962
Guy Lafleur — 1977, 1978

Art Ross Trophy
(for top-scoring player)
Joe Malone — 1918
Edouard "Newsy" Lalonde — 1919, 1921
Howie Morenz — 1928, 1931
Hector "Toe" Blake — 1939
Elmer Lach — 1945, 1948
Bernie Geoffrion — 1955, 1961
Jean Béliveau — 1956
Dickie Moore — 1958, 1959
Guy Lafleur — 1976–78

Vezina Trophy (for top goalie)
George Hainsworth — 1927–29
Bill Durnan — 1944–47, 1949, 1950
Jacques Plante — 1956–60, 1962
Charlie Hodge — 1964, 1966
Lorne "Gump" Worsley — 1966, 1968
Rogie Vachon — 1968
Ken Dryden — 1973, 1976–79
Michel Larocque — 1977–79, 1981
Richard Sevigny — 1981
Denis Herron — 1981
Patrick Roy — 1989, 1990, 1992

James Norris Memorial Trophy (for top defenceman)
Doug Harvey — 1955–58, 1960, 1961
Tom Johnson — 1959
Jacques Laperriere — 1966
Larry Robinson — 1977, 1980
Chris Chelios — 1989

Calder Memorial Trophy
(for top rookie)
John Quilty — 1941
Bernie Geoffrion — 1952
Ralph Backstrom — 1959
Bobby Rousseau — 1962
Jacques Laperriere — 1964
Ken Dryden — 1972

Conn Smythe Trophy
(for most valuable player in the playoffs)
Jean Béliveau — 1965
Serge Savard — 1969
Ken Dryden — 1971
Yvan Cournoyer — 1973

Guy Lafleur — 1977
Larry Robinson — 1978
Bob Gainey — 1979
Patrick Roy — 1986, 1993

Lady Byng Memorial Trophy (for most gentlemanly player)
Toe Blake — 1946
Mats Naslund — 1988

Frank J. Selke Trophy
(for top defensive forward)
Bob Gainey — 1978–81
Guy Carbonneau — 1988, 1989, 1992

Jack Adams Award (for top coach)
Scotty Bowman — 1977
Pat Burns — 1989

William M. Jennings Trophy
(for fewest goals against)
Rick Wamsley, Denis Herron — 1982
Patrick Roy, Brian Hayward — 1987–89
Patrick Roy — 1992

Bill Masterton Memorial Trophy (for most dedicated player)
Claude Provost — 1968
Henri Richard — 1974
Serge Savard — 1979

Lester B. Pearson Award
(for top player as chosen by the players)
Guy Lafleur — 1976–78

SELECTED RECORD HOLDERS

Team Career Records
Most games: Henri Richard (1256)
Most goals: Maurice Richard (544)
Most assists: Guy Lafleur (728)
Most points: Guy Lafleur (1246)
Most shutouts: George Hainsworth (75)

Team Season Records
Most goals: Guy Lafleur and Steve Shutt (60)
Most assists: Peter Mahovlich (82)
Most points: Guy Lafleur (136)
Most shutouts: George Hainsworth (22)

NHL Records
Most Stanley Cup titles: Montreal Canadiens (24 — one Cup won before the creation of the NHL)
Most final series appearances: Montreal Canadiens (32)
Most years in playoffs: Montreal Canadiens (69)
Most shutouts, one season: George Hainsworth (22)
Most overtime goals: Maurice Richard (6)
Most goals, one playoff game: Maurice Richard (5), Newsy Lalonde (5)
Most points, one playoff period: Maurice Richard (4)